HEL I CH

We hope you enjoy this book.
Please return or renew it by the due date.
You can renew it at **www.norfolk.gov.uk/libraries**
or by using our free library app. Otherwise you can
phone **0344 800 8020** - please have your library
card and pin ready.
You can sign up for email reminders too.

NORFOLK COUNTY COUNCIL
LIBRARY AND INFORMATION SERVICE

D0332252

For CP, who always wanted
to read the next bit

OXFORD
UNIVERSITY PRESS

Great Clarendon Street, Oxford OX2 6DP

Oxford University Press is a department of the University of Oxford.
It furthers the University's objective of excellence in research, scholarship,
and education by publishing worldwide. Oxford is a registered trade mark of
Oxford University Press in the UK and in certain other countries

British Library Cataloguing in Publication Data

Data available

ISBN: 978-0-19-277149-0

1 3 5 7 9 10 8 6 4 2

Printed in China

Paper used in the production of this book is a natural,
recyclable product made from wood grown in sustainable forests.

The manufacturing process conforms to the environmental
regulations of the country of origin.

SUPER HAPPY MAGIC FOREST

AND THE HUMONGOUS FUNGUS

MATTY LONG

OXFORD
UNIVERSITY PRESS

THE SUPER HAPPY HEROES

Hoofius (faun)

A delightful mix of pointy and furry bits, Hoofius likes to take on the role of leader of the heroes. He takes questing very seriously and holds nothing but contempt for clothes and personal grooming.

Blossom (unicorn)

A champion frolicker, Blossom is impulsive and likes to live in the moment. His unpredictable nature surprises friends and enemies alike.

He also eats like a horse.

Twinkle (fairy)

The only airborne member of the group, Twinkle is a useful scout and surprisingly strong for her size. She's also easily distracted by anything cute or shiny.

Herbert (gnome)

Rake-wielder and packer of picnics. Questing without Herbert would likely see you lost, hungry, and unable to identify wild flowers.

Trevor (mushroom)

Small, squishy, and great in an omelette, Trevor doesn't seem like your typical hero. Perhaps there is more to this mushroom than we think?

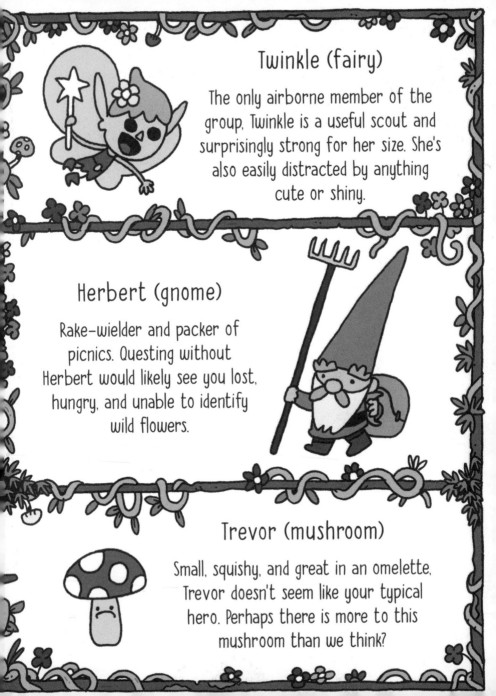

CHAPTER ONE

A LONG-EXPECTED FROLIC

In the middle of nowhere in particular lies the SUPER HAPPY MAGIC FOREST. It is a place of fun and frolics, where rainbows sprout from the ground and ice creams grow on trees. That's right: actual ice creams, in a variety of flavours. Except mint. Nobody likes mint ice cream. You can also get sprinkles and a flake, if you ask nicely. Which you will do because everyone does in the Super Happy Magic Forest. But enough about ice cream! Turn over for a handy visual guide . . .

Don't let the black-and-white pictures fool you. The Super Happy Magic Forest is home to all kinds of colourful characters.

Gnomes.

Has not moved for three hours.

You're IT!

Pixies.

Hee-hee.

Unicorns.

Om nom nom

Today we find the forest in full party mode as the residents prepare to celebrate the Frolic Festival. In a sunny clearing, an elder named Gnomedalf is ready to tell the tale of the beginnings of the Super Happy Magic Forest to a group of wide-eyed youngsters.

Gnomedalf cleared his throat. 'Long have I researched the beginnings of our beloved forest. A forest that came to be when an egg appeared at the end of a majestic triple rainbow. As it hatched, beams of light pierced the cracks and the shell broke away.

 'The Rainbow Dragon   was born!

'She flittered up into the air and opened her mouth, shooting forth not fire but breath of life in seven spectacular hues! The barren land beneath her was transformed with every breath. Mountains and giant mushrooms reached for the sky as flowers unfurled and the very first lollipops sprung from the earth.

'The forest grew and grew. With her work nearly complete, the Rainbow Dragon crafted three mystical crystals, granting them with the power to radiate life, helping the forest to grow and nourish all who would call it home.

'The power of the crystals reached far and wide, and attracted creatures pure of heart to the forest, to live in peace and happiness together.

I baked you a casserole!

I baked YOU BOTH casseroles!

And I baked you a casserole!

'When her work was done, the Rainbow Dragon slept in what we know as the Sacred Glade. After all, it was tiring work. You ever tried breathing a forest? I get tired just tying my shoes. Anyway, where was I? Ah, yes! Every hundred years we honour the Rainbow Dragon with the Frolic Festival.

'We sing and dance and play music until the Rainbow Dragon wakes from her slumber and graces us with her presence.

'She'll usually do a few twirls and spins in the air, just for effect, before imbuing the mystical crystals with new life. Which just helps to keep things ticking over for the next hundred years! Quite remarkable, I'm sure you'll agree. Now, any questions?'

ZzZz...

I'll take that as a no.

But the Rainbow Dragon was nowhere to be seen.

The band played harder.

And everyone frolicked faster.

Just as it looked like they might have to frolic through lunchtime, something appeared in the distance.

It had a long neck and a coiled tail, with unmistakable butterfly wings.

The Rainbow Dragon!

She flew towards the revellers, who cheered her arrival with what little energy they had left. The Rainbow Dragon twisted and spun in the air as the band played, and everyone greeted her movements with a chorus of 'Aaaah!' and 'Ooooh!' and 'AaaaCHOOOO!' (because it was hay fever season).

'NOBODY RUNS FOR THEIR LIVES UNLESS THE COUNCIL OF HAPPINESS SAYS SO!'

shouted Tiddlywink the pixie, a member
of the council, but it was too late.
The frolicking fields were emptying
faster than a gnome's watering can
on a hot summer's day.

They all turned and watched
with mouths open as the dragon
gave one last dizzy twist
before spiralling into
the ground.

CHAPTER TWO

ENTER THE HEROES

Now, it's not as if a sick dragon was the only drama the Super Happy Magic Forest had ever faced. Luckily, for every hiccup, there have always been five brave heroes who have answered the call. Five heroes who always stand together in the face of evil. Five heroes who will always make their voices heard . . .

One way or another, these five friends have always triumphed over any evil afflicting the forest. So they tend to be the go-to choice for all your questing needs.

. . . and Trevor the mushroom.

Today they've been given an urgent task by
the Council of Happiness.

'Where are we going?' asked Blossom, in-
between big mouthfuls of candyfloss.

'To the Sacred Glade to find out what made
the Rainbow Dragon so sick,' replied Hoofius.

'Don't you remember anything that
happened at the Frolic Festival?' said
Herbert.

'Or afterwards, when we were summoned before the Council of Happiness and given this quest?' continued Twinkle. Blossom was too busy pulling splinters out of his tongue to respond.

'You really shouldn't eat the stick as well,' said Trevor.

The Sacred Glade lay deep within the Super Happy Magic Forest. Here the trees grew tallest, enough to keep out the sunlight except for a few cracks in the canopy where the beams burst through. As nobody was usually allowed to enter, it was eerily quiet. And dark.

But the first thing they noticed was the
smell.

'It wasn't me,' said Blossom, worried that the others might jump to conclusions.

'This isn't natural,' said Herbert, covering his nose.

They wandered, a bit lost, through the dense undergrowth of the forest floor, when the quietness of the place was broken by a low gurgling sound, followed by what might well have been a loud belch.

'It came from over there,' whispered Twinkle, pointing towards a mossy verge.

They heard another belching sound, louder this time.

'Sounds like a relative of yours, Blossom,' quipped Trevor.

They clambered up the bank. Whatever was making those noises was on the other side. And judging from the smell, it was probably to blame for making the Rainbow Dragon sick.

Very slowly, they peeked over the top.

Normal mushrooms could grow to be huge in the Super Happy Magic Forest, but not mushroom folk, like Trevor. This one was bigger than any of his kind. And it smelt a lot worse, too.

Trevor leaned over the ridge to get a closer look. As he stared at the super shroom, he lost his balance and toppled over the edge. Mushrooms rolling down hills wasn't an uncommon sight in the Super Happy Magic Forest. Fun is fun, after all. But this was not exactly the time or place.

When Trevor finally came to a halt, two giant red eyes flicked open and stared at him.

'Welcome, puny mushroom! My name is FUNGELLUS. And who might you be?'

'T . . . Trevor.' His voice came out a lot squeakier than he'd hoped.

'T–Trevor is it? Hmmm. I have mushrooms bigger than you growing out of my rear end!' Fungellus chuckled and then coughed, the growths on his side wobbling.

'Listen here. I'm in charge now. The boss! The big cheese! Your forest will wilt under my control. You are pathetic and weak . . . but I could make you POWERFUL. How would you like to join me? We mushrooms could— BELCH—rule all!'

Trevor took a couple of hops back as the monster mushroom began to cough and wheeze.

'Did someone say there was big cheese?' enquired Blossom, as the others caught up with Trevor.

'So . . . you've brought some friends,' said Fungellus. 'And I suppose you're here trying to find out what—BURP— happened to that adorable creature that called this glade home.'

'What did you do to the Rainbow Dragon?' demanded Twinkle. She could be quite threatening, for a fairy. But Fungellus seemed amused.

'It all started when I was a tiny toxic spore,' he said, 'floating on the breeze from a rather different forest not far from here . . .

'. . . I found my way through the cracks in the trees . . .

'... and settled on a damp mossy patch not far from the Rainbow Dragon.

'As it slept, I grew bigger and more toxic.'

'Sheesh. We didn't ask for your life story,' said Trevor, feeling a bit bolder with his friends beside him.

'SO YOU SEE,' boomed Fungellus, talking over the interruption. 'Your precious dragon was breathing in my—BUUURP!—toxic fumes while you fools were dancing in the meadows and making daisy chains!'

As he belched again, a small fluffy orb escaped his mouth and hung in the air.

'Ahhh. Did you see that? The first spore. Soon they will spread my corruption throughout your forest, and you will all bow to my power!'

'Bahaha! You have two choices: you can all leave the forest forever ... or, you can stay here and rot along with it. One thing is certain: Fungellus is in charge now.'

'Who's Fungellus?' asked Blossom, not quite keeping up.

'I AM FUNGELLUS! Now go. And think about what I've said. Especially you, T–Trevor.'

The heroes made their way out of the Sacred Glade, following a trail of jelly beans that Herbert had left on their way in. He was full of clever ideas like that.

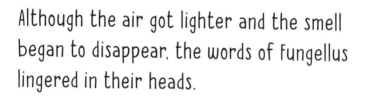

Although the air got lighter and the smell began to disappear, the words of Fungellus lingered in their heads.

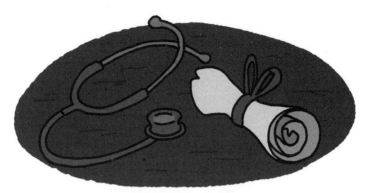

CHAPTER THREE

DOCTOR'S ORDERS

'What did Fungellus mean when he said, "Especially you, T–Trevor"?' asked Twinkle.

Trevor had been quiet on the walk back.

His little mushroom mind was whirring. It wasn't easy being the smallest hero, especially when you had no arms or legs. Could Fungellus really make Trevor big and powerful? He thought it best to keep that offer a secret, at least for now.

37

'Not sure. Maybe he just wants all the other mushrooms to leave the forest? Perhaps Fungellus sees us as competition.'

They all stopped and looked at Trevor suspiciously, who in response tried to puff up his body as much as possible to appear big and tough.

When they finally walked out into bright sunshine, a butterfly appeared, huffing and puffing.

There was no time for chit-chat. Denise led them to a house where the Council of Happiness was huddled around a table. Consisting of Tiddlywink, Sunshine, Butterfly Horse, and Admin Bunny, it was they who were trusted to make big decisions in times of crisis. Below them the Rainbow Dragon lay, motionless.

It was Tiddlywink who spoke first, as he usually did.

'Ahhh, there you are! Where in the name of bubblegum have you been?' he huffed, going a bit red in the process.

'We were investigating the Sacred Glade. Like you told us!' said Hoofius.

'Never mind that! We think we know a way to save the Rainbow Dragon!' chirped Tiddlywink. 'Shroomsworth! Where are you?'

A mushroom emerged out of a back room, whistling as he walked. It was Dr Shroomsworth. Whether or not he was actually a real doctor was up for debate, but one day a mushroom decided to put on a white coat and stethoscope, and

everyone just kind of went along with it.
He was all they had.

'Greetings, friends, and welcome to my
home,' he said, before taking a glance at
the Rainbow Dragon and shaking his head,
all the while making tutting sounds. It
went on for some time.

'How long does she have, Doctor?' asked
Herbert at last.

'Hard to say,' said Shroomsworth. 'I mostly deal with frolicking-related aches and pains. But believe me, this is one poorly customer.'

'For goodness' sake, Shroomsworth! Get to the part about the antidote!' Tiddlywink looked ready to explode.

Shroomsworth cleared his throat. 'I've come up with a list of ingredients that, when mixed together, should be enough to revive the Rainbow Dragon,' he said, as Admin Bunny stepped forward and handed the list to Hoofius.

Here you are. I trust you'll look after it. The illustrations took me quite a while.

Revive The Rainbow Dragon!

by AdminBunny

A (Pot) of **Sprite Jam**

Hugberry Juice

Five-leaf Clover

BLUE Candyfloss

Unicorn Poop

'UNICORN POOP!?'

squealed Blossom.

'Indeed,' said Dr Shroomsworth. 'Unicorn poop is incredibly rare, but is absolutely bursting with magical healing properties.'

'And how do you know this, Doctor?' asked Trevor, suspiciously.

'There will be plenty of time to question the doctor on his strange practices once the Rainbow Dragon is fit and healthy again!' said Tiddlywink. 'We need you heroes to find these ingredients throughout the forest. It should be a piece of cake for you.'

'An ingredients-gathering quest! How wonderful!' chimed Herbert.

'When do we get the piece of cake?' asked Blossom.

'Nobody is getting any cake,' replied the pixie. 'It was a figure of speech. Now, get out there and find those ingredients!'

'NOT SO FAST!'

They all jumped in surprise. Tiddlywink's hat nearly hit the ceiling. In the corner of the room was Gnomedalf, broom in hand.

You left the door unlocked.

'What are you doing here?' Tiddlywink asked, arranging his headgear back in place.

'I'm Shroomsworth's next appointment,' said the old gnome, rubbing his back with his free hand. 'Besides, haven't you forgotten something very important? *The Sacred Glade*. These brave heroes have journeyed there and back. Don't you want to know what they have to say about it?'

Tiddlywink went his trademark shade of red.

Hoofius told them all about Fungellus and his plans to corrupt the entire forest and take control, as Admin Bunny busily wrote everything down.

Gnomedalf listened carefully, but it was hard to know what he made of it all beneath his bushy eyebrows and beard.

'This is most troubling,' he said at last. 'Our forest is being poisoned from the inside out. How can we possibly overcome such evil?'

'Maybe . . . we could take Fungellus some ice cream?' offered Butterfly Horse. 'When I'm feeling like a grumpy-guts, I have some ice cream and that always makes me happy!'

That'll do the trick!

'With the greatest respect to the Council of Happiness, we can't go around giving everyone who wants to destroy our home ice cream!' said Gnomedalf, his voice rising. 'But . . . there is a chance that if we can revive the Rainbow Dragon to full strength with an antidote made from these ingredients, then the power of her life-giving breath could purify the forest and drive Fungellus out once and for all.'

The Rainbow Dragon let out a distressed whimper.

Hoofius clenched his fists. 'Then that is what we'll do!'

'I'd best pack a picnic,' said Herbert.

CHAPTER FOUR

THE HUNT FOR SPRITE JAM

With a picnic prepared and packed in record time, the heroes were ready for the quest. Hoofius scanned the list they'd been given and smiled.

'It makes sense to start with an easy one. Blossom, have you got . . . anything for us?'

I'll let you know when it's ready.

'Probably best you keep it in for now,' said Trevor. 'We don't want to be carrying it around with us.'

'How about sprite jam?' suggested Herbert, keen to change the subject.

Sprite jam is made from the sweetest berries of the Super Happy Magic Forest, by the tiniest hands.

The elusive sprites gather the best berries they can find and mix them all up in little pots using their secret recipe. Once they're done, they hide the pots around the forest for folk to find. Usually, once a pot of sprite jam has been located, one thing leads to another, and all of a sudden you've got yourself a picnic.

'Where do we look for it? It could be anywhere!' said Twinkle.

'Ah, not to the trained sprite jam hunter!' replied Herbert, rummaging in his bag for his magnifying glass.
'Follow me!'

Hoofius wasn't impressed.

'Herbert! I thought you were an expert at finding this stuff.'

'Well . . . I wouldn't say *expert*. But I earned my sprite jam badge in the Super Happy Scouts.'

'Wasn't that over a hundred years ago?' joked Trevor.

But something had caught Herbert's attention.

It was Blossom.

And he was licking a tree.

Hee-hee, that tickles!

'Blossom! Can't you lick trees after we've saved the forest?' Hoofius groaned.

'Hold on just a moment, Hoofius.' Herbert paced over to the tree and raised his magnifying glass. 'Just as I suspected! Look—Blossom is licking a dab of sprite jam! Often the sprites will leave little clues when there is a pot nearby.'

Herbert had a spring in his step. He busily examined the area before stopping to investigate a thicket.

The sprites seemed delighted that their jam had been found and fluttered off into the undergrowth as Herbert reached through to pick up the jar. 'I hope the whole quest is this easy!' he said, holding it aloft. The friends celebrated their capture of the first ingredient as only heroes do . . .

VICTORY POSE!

CHAPTER FIVE
RIDDLES ON CLOVER HILL

'Are you going to finish all that jam?' asked Blossom, as the heroes headed off to find the next ingredient.

'The sprite jam is for the Rainbow Dragon, remember?' replied Herbert.

'Oh . . . yeah,' said Blossom thoughtfully, licking his lips. He'd got a taste for the stuff now.

'Here we are!' said Hoofius. 'Clover Hill. There must be a five-leaf clover on it somewhere.'

'Last one up smells like Fungellus!' called Twinkle, racing ahead. Trevor sighed. Mushrooms weren't the quickest going *up* hills.

Once at the top, the heroes began examining each clover for five leaves. A boring old four-leaf clover just wouldn't do.

ZzZz . . .

They hadn't been looking long when they heard a rustling noise coming from nearby.

'Did anyone hear that?' asked Hoofius. They all sat as still as they could.

Rustle, rustle.

'There it is again!' he whispered. Blossom crawled over to the others, looking startled. 'Something just brushed past my belly!'

'Over there!' cried Herbert. They could see the clover shaking as something snaked and moved beneath it.

'Didn't Fungellus say something about corrupting the forest?' asked Twinkle.

'Be on your guard!' said Hoofius, with a slight tremble in his voice. 'There's no telling what horrors Fungellus may have unleashed upon us.'

'WHAAAH! GET IT AWAY!'

shrieked Blossom, flailing his arms.

Herbert sighed. 'Calm down, Blossom. It's just Pappy. Hello there, Pappy.'

The leprechaun skipped up to them. Twinkle frowned. 'Did you really have to spook us like that?'

'Spook? Who's spooked? It's a fine morning! The sun's shining! Everything's grand!' He did a little jig on the spot and clapped his hands together. It was pretty annoying, all in all.

'If this is part of Fungellus's plan to make us leave the forest, it's working,' said Trevor.

'What brings you all the way up Clover Hill?' enquired Pappy.

'We need a five-leaf clover, and quickly!' replied Hoofius. 'We need to save the Rainbow Dragon. It's an important quest!'

'Ah, yes. I heard about that. Well . . . lucky for you, I can find one with a click of the fingers!'

Pappy snapped his fingers together, and a five-leaf clover unfurled in his palm, drawing gasps and a round of applause from the heroes.

'Wow, that's great!' said Hoofius, reaching out to take it.

'Not so fast, my fur-legged friend!'

Pappy closed his palm. 'You have to riddle with me first! It's the leprechaun code.'

Leprechaun code?

Yup. Paragraph twenty-six.

'We don't have time to read all that! Just tell us the riddle.'

Pappy tucked the scroll away and cleared his throat.

A cloud for a head, a stick for a leg, sometimes blue, mostly pink, take a bite and feel it shrink!

One-legged cloud?

Pink cloud head?

Shrinky stick!

Bitey blue cloud!

Am I close?

No.

'It's candyfloss,' said Trevor.

'Ding, ding! Right you are!' Pappy did another excited jig.

'Can we please have the clover now?' Hoofius groaned, eager to keep the quest moving.

'Of course. But you have to catch me first!'

'WHAT!?'

'It's the leprechaun code!'

Pappy whipped out the scroll once more. Hoofius snatched it from him and inspected it closely.

68

'Let's see here. Turnips . . . potatoes . . . gold polish . . . HEY! This isn't a leprechaun code. It's your shopping list!'

'Catch me if you can!' cried Pappy, as he disappeared into a mass of clover.

'In a way, you've got to admire his dedication to the art of being very annoying,' said Trevor. But Hoofius was in no mood for it.

'We've got more chance of catching him if we split up,' he said.

And so that's what they did. Or at least, they tried to. Catching a leprechaun on his home turf is not easy.

As the heroes began to tire of pouncing on thin air, they had a breakthrough. Pappy, having easily evaded the taller and more airborne members of the group, clattered into Trevor and sent them both tumbling down Clover Hill.

They rolled and rolled, down through a hedgerow and out of sight.

CHAPTER SIX
THE BAD THINGS

When they finally came to a halt, Trevor was upside down. And sinking.

Well, this is a shame.

'Ahhh! Sticky sinking mud!' cried Pappy, struggling to get free. They found themselves in a pond—or what once would have been. The water had become dark and gloopy. And it didn't smell nice. Around the edges, unfamiliar vines and nettles curled out from the darkened earth.

Trevor watched as the leprechaun flapped about in the mud, sinking deeper.

'GRAB ON!' came a voice from nearby.

Herbert's rake poked through the greenery surrounding the pond. Pappy reached out an arm, clasped the rake, and was slowly dragged through the mud and out of sight.

'Don't mind me,' called Trevor. 'I'm perfectly fine here. No need to rush.' The gloop had nearly reached his eyes. The rake appeared again.

GRAB ON!

There might be a problem with that idea.

The rake withdrew and promptly reappeared, handle first.

'Too far away!' shouted Trevor. It hovered closer and closer until it poked him in the face.

'Argh!'

He wrapped his mouth around as tight as he could and was slowly lifted out of the pond to safety.

'Would you look at these stains?' said Pappy, examining his outfit as the pair lay dripping on the grass. 'I'll have to add new boots and trousers to my shopping list.'

'Ahem!'

Hoofius stood over the leprechaun, arm outstretched and palm open. And he wasn't helping him up.

Pappy produced a five-leaf clover, with a lot less theatre than before.

Soon afterwards, the heroes found themselves beside a running stream, where Herbert put his travel-sized watering can to good use.

But Trevor wasn't in the mood for Herbert's humour. A bigger, more powerful mushroom wouldn't have needed rescuing in the first place, he thought, remembering his talk with Fungellus.

As Trevor shook off the last muddy drips, a butterfly appeared before them. It was Denise, the Council of Happiness messenger.

'Heroes! I'm so glad I . . . found you!' She was out of breath again. They sure worked hard, these butterflies. 'Something terrible . . . is happening at Pixie Village! Please . . . please help!'

Hoofius leapt to his feet. Well, hooves.

'We're on our way!'

'MY BABY! MY BABY! WHO WILL SAVE PIXIE JUNIOR?' wailed a mother pixie in distress, as a large prickly bramble coiled around her house.

Blossom burst into action. He squeezed through the front door (pixie houses are a bit on the small side) and rushed upstairs. Soon the windows swung open and Blossom dangled the baby pixie out in triumph.

A crowd had gathered below, and they cheered and clapped at the sight, without noticing the bramble stretching around the roof and sneaking inside.

One of the prickles caught Blossom on the rear. He yelped in surprise and dropped the baby out of the window.

If Trevor hadn't been standing directly below, the heroes may have had a bigger problem than Fungellus on their hands.

The pixie baby bounced off Trevor's foamy head and into the grateful arms of its mother.

The crowd **gasped** and then **cheered**
again as the baby landed safely.

But the prickly plant wasn't done yet. It
snapped away from the pixie house and
lashed out at Trevor.

Herbert hacked at the bramble, and it let go of Trevor. Down he dropped, until an outstretched arm broke his fall.

Sensing defeat, the monstrous plant retreated into the earth.

'And stay there!' cried Herbert as the onlookers cheered once again.

'What's all this brouhaha?' came the voice of Tiddlywink as the Council of Happiness entered the village. 'And what are these things?'

'DON'T TOUCH THOSE!' came a cry.

Tiddlywink snatched a spore out of the air to examine it, before turning a particular shade of green and running to the nearest pond.

'Those bad things floated into Pixie Village and started turning the ground and the plants all horrible,' sobbed a pixie.

'And if someone touches one, it makes them very sick!' added another.

'Yes . . . I can see that,' replied Tiddlywink, wiping his mouth.

'The pond at Clover Hill . . . it must have been affected by these spores,' said Hoofius. 'Fungellus threatened to spread the corruption. It has begun!'

'Then you'd best get a move on with finding those ingredients!' said Tiddlywink. 'We've left Dr Shroomsworth with the Rainbow Dragon. She seems to be feeling worse. But then, so would I if I had to hang around

Shroomsworth all day!' Tiddlywink chuckled at his own joke, but his tender stomach clearly wasn't up to the task, and he made a beeline for the nearest bush.

'In all seriousness,' continued Sunshine, as the sounds of the pixie being sick filled the air, 'we must make haste. With every second that passes, the poor Rainbow Dragon becomes ever more weak.'

Blossom's stomach let out a deafening grumble.

'Can it wait until after lunch?' he said.

CHAPTER SEVEN
A TALE OF TWO BELLIES

'Behind every great quest, is an even greater picnic!' Herbert declared, handing out the paper plates.

'You say that every time!' laughed Twinkle.

Despite the doom and gloom, even heroes need to eat lunch. They had found an agreeable spot on a hill to rest and eat— one that wasn't affected by spores or riddling leprechauns. It was all Blossom could do to keep from drooling over everything as he watched Herbert produce each part of the picnic from his backpack and place it on the blanket.

As he did so, an apple escaped his grip and rolled all the way down the hill.

Whoopsie daisy . . .

I'll get it. Maybe I can rescue something for a change.

The events of the quest were weighing on Trevor's mind. Fungellus had called him pathetic and weak, and it was hard not to feel like that when you needed help as often as Trevor did. And he'd only saved that pixie baby by accident, truth be told.

I'm not strong enough to be a hero, Trevor thought.

As he searched the undergrowth for the wayward apple, something else caught his attention. It sounded like muffled cries for help, coming from a clearing nearby.

Slowly, Trevor approached.

At the centre of the clearing was a large plant he didn't recognize.

He heard the cries again, louder this time. Were they coming from inside?

Trevor scanned the plant suspiciously from top to bottom as it stood completely still.

And then he noticed the rotten ground beneath it.

As he turned to hop away, a vine **snapped** out of the earth and whipped him up into the air.

The last thing Trevor expected after being eaten was a warm welcome, but these were strange times indeed.

'Uh-oh. This doesn't look good.' Trevor peered around the dark belly of the plant at the other mushrooms.

'Trevor! You have to get us out of here!' It was Marvin. Trevor knew him from chess club. 'This plant . . . it's gobbling up mushroom folk. Pretty soon there will be none of us left!'

Something caught Trevor's eye. 'Hang on . . . if this plant likes eating mushrooms, then what is Buttercup the unicorn doing here?'

Buttercup's face poked out from amongst the fungi. 'I just wanted to get my frisbee back.'

Trevor thought on that for a moment. 'Do you still have the frisbee?' he asked.

'Sure!' Buttercup started rummaging around, and mushrooms rolled away as she thrust her arm in the air, Frisbee in hoof.

'Great!' said Trevor, feeling a plan coming together. 'Throw it as hard as you can!'

Buttercup launched the Frisbee, and it spun and bounced off the walls. The plant wriggled and snorted, like it was being tickled from inside.

It heaved and rolled back, before sneezing the contents of its belly all over the forest floor.

Trevor gave a long sigh as Marvin hopped over to him.

'What's the matter, Trevor? We're
freeeee!
I fancy some chess. Pawn to C4!'

'Don't you see?' said Trevor. 'We mushrooms are hopeless! We're no more useful than pawns ourselves. We'd never have got out of there without Buttercup. I can't even throw a Frisbee!'

'But it was your idea . . . You're a real hero!'

'I don't feel like one.' Trevor hung his head and stared at the ground. 'Real heroes don't need to be rescued three times before they've even had lunch.'

Fungellus's offer of power crept temptingly into Trevor's head once again as Hoofius, Herbert, and Twinkle rushed into the clearing.

'There you are!' cried Hoofius. 'We heard a big sneezing sound, and . . .' he paused and looked around at the mushrooms, rolling on the floor in sticky plant-belly goo.

'Don't ask,' said Trevor. 'Where's Blossom?'

'Guarding the picnic,' said Herbert.

Trevor's face dropped. 'You left BLOSSOM to guard the PICNIC?'

It wasn't quite Pixie Village levels of chaos, but it was close.

Well, at least he didn't eat the blanket.

Herbert ran to his backpack and began sifting through in a panic.

'It's not here!' he cried. Blossom let out a belch. They all turned.

Next to Blossom was an empty pot of sprite jam.

CHAPTER EIGHT
HUG IT OUT

'The flavours . . . they were like nothing I've ever tasted. It was useless to resist!'

If Blossom was sorry, it didn't seem like it.

'Now what do we do?' cried Twinkle. 'We needed that jam to save the Rainbow Dragon!'

'But on the bright side, at least we'll get that unicorn poop sooner,' said Trevor.

A butterfly fluttered into view. It looked like it could collapse from exhaustion at any moment.

'Now is not a good time, Denise!' said Hoofius.

Heroes! I have terrible, terrible news! The Council of Happiness has...has... DISAPPEARED!

'Yes,' panted Denise. 'And even more spores have been spotted in the forest. Please hurry . . . you're all we have left!'

Hoofius consulted the list as Herbert hurriedly packed up the remnants of the picnic. Even in these crazy times, you wouldn't catch a gnome littering.

'Hugberry juice!' said Hoofius. 'We will have to deal with the sprite jam later.'

'Hugberries are so cute!' said Twinkle. 'And I know just where to find 'em!'

All the fairies knew about the Great
Hugberry Bush. It sat in the middle of a
heart–shaped lake, and as such, it was
fairies who were best suited to harvesting
the delicious berry juice.

POPULAR FAIRY
HANG-OUT

Giggle

Twinkle volunteered herself for the task,
and Herbert handed her a flask to collect
their next ingredient.

Over the lake she flew.

The hugberries hadn't had any visitors for a
while—no doubt due to the chaos unfolding
in the forest—and were keen to offload
some of their sweet, sweet berry juice.

A little too keen.

The other heroes watched eagerly as Twinkle flew back over the lake.

She hovered in the air beside them, soaked from head to toe and dripping hugberry juice over the grass.

Looks like they were happy to see you.

Hmph!

'So . . . did you . . . get any hugberry juice?' asked Hoofius, nervously.

Twinkle dropped the empty flask at their feet. 'No. Unless you count the juice I'm WEARING!'

'Now, now, Twinkle,' said Herbert. 'All might not be lost. Just try to stay still.' He positioned the flask underneath her to catch the juicy drips.

'I don't get it,' said Twinkle. 'The hugberries were all mean! Something was making them act crazy.'

'This just gets worse by the minute,' Hoofius said, scratching his head. 'First the Council of Happiness goes missing; now hugberries are attacking anyone who goes near. When will this madness end?'

'When we save the Rainbow Dragon and she blasts Fungellus away!' shouted Blossom.

'That's the spirit, Blossom. And look!' Herbert held up a full flask of juice. 'One step closer!'

CHAPTER NINE

NEW CRAZE IN TOWN

Twinkle had just about dried off by the time the five friends closed in on Candyfloss Cave in search of their next ingredient: the rare blue candyfloss.

'AHHHHHHH!'

A pixie rushed by, followed by a whole host of panic-stricken creatures. The heroes became aware of a chant in the distance.

109

'TEAR IT DOWN!

TEAR IT DOWN!

TEAR IT DOWN!'

The chant got louder as they approached.

'Twinkle! Watch out!' Herbert jumped and pulled at Twinkle's leg as a cluster of spores drifted over her head. They looked different from before: redder. And more angry.

'TEAR IT DOWN!

TEAR IT DOWN!

TEAR IT DOWN!'

Such a chant had not been heard in the Super Happy Magic Forest since Tiddlywink erected a statue of himself next to Candyfloss Cave.

'What has got into them!?' cried Herbert.
But the madness was all around.

'Errrr guys . . . a little help?'

The heroes turned
to find a pixie using
Trevor's head as
a trampoline.

As they moved to help,
an ice cream flew
into the pixie's face and sent him
sprawling. A bunny ran away, cackling.

'We have to keep moving!' said Hoofius. 'Or
we'll get caught up in this!'

But it was too late.

The group that moments ago had been trying to uproot an ice cream tree now had their sights set on the heroes, and they had a catchy new chant to boot.

'Spore them! Spore them! Spore them!'

came the cry. A gnome had been catching spores in a butterfly net and was heading towards them.

'Are heroes allowed to run away!?' Blossom asked.

'I think so!' cried Trevor from down the path, knowing he needed the head start. As they fled the scene with the spore-crazed mob in hot pursuit, a voice called out to them.

Pssst! Heroes! Over here! Quickly!

They dived into the burrow and soon heard the angry mob pounding past the entrance.

A few moments passed in nervous silence.

The bunny peered out of the burrow.
'We should be safe here,' he said at last,
satisfied that nobody had seen them.

'They didn't get you, did they?' He hopped
over and started inspecting the heroes in
a panic. They seemed to be spore-free.

'What's going on out there?' gasped Hoofius,
trying to get his breath back.

'Those new spores floated in, and they're
making everyone they cling to go bananas!'

'The spores have . . . changed?' Hoofius
asked, his eyes wide.

'Uh-huh!' said the bunny. 'I'd take the puking any day over this.'

'The hugberries!' said Twinkle. 'The spores must have got to them too!'

The bunny shook his head in pity, but then perked up.

'Where are my manners? My name is Nibbles, and I live here in the Bunny Tunnels. I know who you all are! Please come with me. I have someone who wishes to speak with you.'

Nibbles guided them through a spacious network of tunnels, arriving at a door. He knocked. 'Enter!' came the reply.

The heroes walked in and all spoke at once:

'Admin Bunny!?'

'We thought you were missing!' The heroes were glad to see at least *one* of the Council of Happiness was okay.

'Not quite,' came the response. 'But the others are. We got separated when that new spore wave hit, and I went into hiding. How fares the quest?'

The heroes filled her in on everything, but neglected to mention the part about Blossom gobbling the sprite jam. They had a reputation to uphold, after all.

Fluffy sighed, and her ears sagged. 'This is all going to result in so much paperwork.'

'Nibbles said you wanted to see us?' enquired Hoofius, trying to take her mind off the admin.

'Indeed! Please forgive my . . . sudden touch of melodrama.' She sat up and straightened her tie. 'I received some intel on our foe, Fungellus. It would appear that he is some kind of super mushroom. So super, in fact, that he produces far too many spores, and simply *has* to keep releasing them!'

'How is *that* supposed to help us?' asked Twinkle.

Fluffy shrugged. 'I'm sure you heroes will find a way to use such knowledge to your advantage. But be sure that you do. We lost a good butterfly to get hold of it. Oh, and one more thing . . .'

She reached into a satchel by the desk and pulled out a pot of sprite jam.

'*More* sprite jam? What does that mean?' asked Fluffy, suspicious.

'Nothing!' said Twinkle. 'Nothing at all!'

Fluffy frowned, picked up her papers, and gave her glasses a nudge. 'Well then, I hate to bring this meeting to a close, but I have a budget report due on Monday. Nibbles will see you out. The Bunny Tunnels stretch right to the entrance of the Candyfloss Cave. Good luck, heroes. We are all depending on you.'

They thanked her and turned to leave.

'And one more thing!' called Admin Bunny. 'If you see my colleagues on the Council . . . tell them I'm safe and sound.'

CHAPTER TEN
FIVE GO TO CANDYFLOSS CAVE

The heroes emerged from the Bunny Tunnels in a buoyant mood. They were just two ingredients away from saving the Rainbow Dragon.

Candyfloss Cave loomed in front of them. Blossom had been looking forward to this part of the quest. He knew the cave like the back of his hoof.

But the blue candyfloss
could only be reached
by delving deep into the
cave. And only Blossom
knew how to get to it.

The heroes paced through Candyfloss Cave, without stopping to sample its sticky pink interior. It wasn't as fun when the forest was teetering on the brink of destruction.

'It's . . . very quiet in here,' said Twinkle, nervously. 'I hope Blossom is okay.'

'He'll be fine,' said Trevor. 'Probably eating his way through all the blue candyfloss as we speak.'

They walked a bit further, where the path split in different directions.

Hoofius had had enough. He cupped his hands around his mouth and took a deep breath.

'BLOOOOSSSSOOOOOOM!'

His voice **echoed** through the caverns, causing a few bits of candyfloss to dislodge and fall silently to the ground around them.

But there was no response from Blossom.

As Hoofius tried again, something struck him on the back of the head.

BLOOOSSAH!

The heroes swivelled to face their attacker.

It was the Council of Happiness.

And they didn't look happy.

'They're all covered in crazy spores!' gasped
Twinkle.

'Well, well, well,' chimed Tiddlywink, tossing a ball of candyfloss up and down in his palm. 'What do we have here?'

'Looks like trouble, if you ask me,' said Sunshine, turning and spitting on the ground.

'Yeah . . . trouble,' said Butterfly Horse, cracking her hooves like things were about to get physical. What on earth were they planning to do?

'Back off, Tiddlywink!' warned Hoofius. 'We're trying to save the Rainbow Dragon, remember?'

'Ha! That won't be necessary. Change of plans, you see. The Council have decided that we are, in fact, the real heroes around here! We will save the forest . . . by handing it over to FUNGELLUS! Now, give us the ingredients!'

The renegade council members advanced, tearing off chunks of candyfloss and rolling them into balls to throw.

The heroes did the same, and the two sides stared each other down, daring each other to make the first move.

He heaved the giant candyfloss ball over the ledge.

The heroes, who were more than used to Blossom's recklessness, dived for cover as Tiddlywink and his fellow council members watched in **horror** as the ball **grew larger** over them.

It collapsed over their heads, a blanket of sticky blue deliciousness.

'Now's our chance!' cried Hoofius to the others. 'Grab some and move out!'

They darted past the enveloped council, picking up some candyfloss for the quest as they made their escape. Blossom wasn't far behind, wondering what all the fuss was about.

He paused for a moment as he passed by the stricken council.

The heroes rushed out into the open air, palms full of blue candyfloss.

'Marvellous timing, Blossom!' said Herbert, catching his breath. 'A second later, and there might have been fisticuffs!'

He produced an empty jar from his backpack, and the heroes eagerly stuffed the candyfloss into it.

They were nearly there.

CHAPTER ELEVEN
DROPPINGS GALORE

'How much longer is this going to take?' mumbled Hoofius. Blossom had certainly been gone a while.

'I'm starting to see why unicorn poop is so rare,' said Trevor.

A few minutes later, Blossom reappeared with the final ingredient.

'Do we still need to do the victory pose?'
asked Twinkle.

'Maybe we should just get all these
ingredients to Shroomsworth right away,'
said Hoofius. The others willingly agreed.

They set off for Shroomsworth's place,
careful not to touch any drifting spores

or be seen by anyone else who might give them trouble. They arrived at the doctor's house safely and knocked on his door.

'There you are! At last. Come in, quickly now!' cried Shroomsworth, glancing nervously around.

They shuffled into Shroomsworth's house, and he bolted the doors behind them.

'Sorry to rush you,' the doctor said. 'But I've been a bit on edge since some rowdy gnomes egged my house.'

The heroes turned to face him and gasped.

What?

'You're . . . covered in spores!'

The heroes took a couple of steps back.

'Oh, those things? Can't seem to shake
them off. And believe me, I've tried.'

'You're not . . . feeling sick? Or going crazy?'
asked Twinkle.

Shroomsworth shook his head. 'Nope. Your
trusted doctor is still of sound mind and
stomach. Now, you have the ingredients,
I hope?'

They handed them over, and he
disappeared into a back room to mix them
all together.

The heroes waited with the Rainbow Dragon. Twinkle stroked her neck as she lay still, whimpering.

After a while, Shroomsworth emerged with the antidote precariously balanced on his head.

'Spray it all over the Rainbow Dragon's body,' he said. 'But be careful not to get any in the eyes. I don't need another lawsuit.'

Hoofius did as he was told, and they waited in anticipation. Her tail flicked out, and the Rainbow Dragon opened her eyes. Her wings stiffened and beat lightly. She cooed and raised herself up, wings beating faster as she took to the air. The Rainbow Dragon hovered above them as glitter danced off her wings and lightly dusted the room. They all watched in amazement for the ten seconds where it looked like everything had gone to plan.

And then she fell back to earth with a THUD.

'Ah,' said Shroomsworth. 'Well, I guess you can't win them all.'

The heroes stared at the Rainbow Dragon, mouths agape.

'W–w–why isn't it working?' stammered Hoofius, feeling a bit faint.

'Hard to say,' said Shroomsworth. 'Maybe the mixture wasn't quite right. I did use a lot of vinegar. But let's not dwell on the negatives. We gave it a good go.'

'Then that's it. We failed. The Super Happy Magic Forest is done for.' A single tear rolled down Hoofius's cheek.

'ALL IS NOT LOST!'

Everyone jumped. In the corner of the room was Gnomedalf, broom in hand.

'How do you keep getting in here?' demanded Shroomsworth, looking more than a little ruffled.

'Never mind that now, Doctor,' said the old gnome, rising to his feet. 'I have been deep in research and, as a result, feared that the antidote might not be enough to revive the Rainbow Dragon. And so it has proved. This can only mean one thing: the Rainbow Dragon created the forest and, as such, her life is bound to that of the forest. When it suffers, she suffers too.'

'But that would mean the only way to make her better is to . . .' Twinkle trailed off, as realization took hold.

'. . . destroy Fungellus yourselves,' finished
Gnomedalf.

There was a long silence.

'Well, good luck with that,' chimed
Shroomsworth, disappearing once more into
the back room. 'Feel free to pop around
afterwards for a complimentary check-up.'

The heroes trudged outside as the door was
bolted tight behind them.

And that's when they saw it.

'SPORE CLOUD!' they cried, and
Hoofius turned to thump on Shroomsworth's
door.

'Shroomsworth! Let us in!'

'Ha, no chance!' came the response. 'You can
egg my house all you want!'

'No! Shroomsworth, it's us! The heroes!
Please . . .'

But it was already too late.

The little puffs of evil swarmed them and
clung on tight, and one by one the heroes
dropped
    to
     the
      ground.

146

CHAPTER TWELVE
MARCH OF THE MUSHROOMS

Trevor realized he was alive when he felt an itching sensation on his mushroom head. A *spore*. But there was no time to think about that now. He hopped over to the others, who lay slumped around him. None of them moved.

'No . . . they can't be!' His lip began to tremble.

Blossom snored loudly.

Trevor tried to wake his friends, but they wouldn't budge. The spores clung on tight. Fungellus must have changed them again, and this time they induced sleep. But why was Trevor okay? He remembered the spores on Shroomsworth. It all began to make sense.

'Mushrooms are immune to the spores!' he cried. He began hopping away, as other fungi poked their heads above ground. Marvin was one of them. 'Trevor! Where are you going?'

'I'm going to finish this! For my friends, for the forest, and for all of us mushrooms who are tired of not feeling like we're good enough! Or at least, that's the plan.'

'Errr . . . I'm with you!' cried Marvin, hopping behind. Before long, others joined in. It became a mushroom conga line the likes of which hadn't been seen since the earliest Frolic Festivals.

And it was heading towards the Sacred Glade.

'So. You have—BELCH—returned, T–Trevor!
And you've brought some other measly
specimens with you!'

Fungellus still sat in a pool of gloop, drooling
and wheezing just like before. But now
countless spores drifted around him, and
even speaking was enough to force more
out of his mouth.

He produces far too many spores, and
simply has to keep releasing them. Admin
Bunny's words echoed in Trevor's head.
Fungellus spoke again.

'Where are your friends from—hic—
before? Too tired to join you? Bahaha! You
Snooze, you lose!'

Trevor gulped. *It's my turn to save them.*

'Perhaps they can't hurt you,' grumbled Fungellus, irritated that his secret was out. 'But they could *help* you. Join me, and my spores will power you up to new levels of size and strength like nothing you've—BELCH—ever known! Don't you want to know what that feels like?'

Trevor remembered the times he had felt weak and helpless during the quest, always relying on his friends. He glanced around at the other mushrooms and knew they were relying on him. Suddenly, it felt like real strength wasn't all about being big and powerful.

'Trevor! Trevor!' Marvin was whispering frantically at him. 'What do we do?'

'It's true . . . we are weak,' said Trevor at last, turning to Fungellus. 'But we can be strong . . . TOGETHER!'

A cheer erupted from the band of mushrooms, and they bobbed up and down in excitement.

'FOOLS!' boomed Fungellus. 'Then allow me to show you—BURP—what you're missing!'

The ground trembled beneath them, and the cheers turned to panic. Large shapes emerged from the earth to form a barrier around Fungellus.

Mushrooms.

Bad mushrooms.

'My spores can't hurt you. But these might!'
chuckled Fungellus. 'I call them the Bad
Caps. Grew them myself, in case I needed to
enforce my ideas for this forest in a more . . .
physical fashion. It is time for you to learn
the true strength of—BELCH—mushroom
kind!'

The Bad Caps advanced towards Trevor and
the others, hissing and growling.

Follow me!

Quite what a mushroom-on-mushroom
brawl looks like we may never know. Because
in that moment, Trevor jumped. He jumped
on the Bad Caps, and bounced into the air.

Trevor spun over the Bad Caps and on to the **humongous** head of Fungellus himself. The others followed. They didn't all nail the landing, and some missed altogether.

IT WAS AN HONOUR TO SERVE YOUuuu.

But there were enough.

'NO! GET OFF! PUNY FOOLS!'

Fungellus began to panic. He thrashed about, trying to shake off the shrooms. But he was too big and slow.

He began sinking down into his own gloop, under the weight of so many mushrooms.

The last spores escaped his mouth as it dipped below the surface. The giant shroom went still.

Is that it? Bit of an anticlimax.

Give it a moment. Things might be about to get interesting.

The mushrooms waited, nervously exchanging glances. Trevor knew it all came down to this.

A shudder. And then another one. Clogged up with spores, Fungellus began to inflate, larger and larger.

'What's happening?' cried Marvin, unable to see what was going on below the giant head of Fungellus.

'You might want to hold on for this bit,' said Trevor. 'Prepare for lift off!'

For a moment, everything seemed still.

And then
Fungellus
exploded.

Trevor opened his eyes. He remembered the journey up and the incredible view . . . but everything was a bit fuzzy after that.

'Marvin! What's that sticking out of your head?'

'Oh. I landed in a tree. But I'm fine! These foamy tops are like natural crash helmets.'

Trevor smiled, and then remembered the other heroes, and the Rainbow Dragon.

It was time to leave the Sacred Glade.

CHAPTER THIRTEEN
THE AFTER-PARTY

Trevor rounded up the mushrooms that lay scattered around their landing zone. Not all of them that had made the journey halfway to orbit were accounted for, but they'd check the trees later for any stragglers. A few carried bruises and other interesting things lodged in their tops. Shroomsworth was certainly going to have his hands full.

All around them, spores fell from the sky and shrivelled up on the ground, as the toxic energy of Fungellus began to fade away. There was no sign of the Bad Caps. But then, they were well within the blast radius. You might need Herbert's magnifying glass to find any trace of them now. Trevor shuddered. 'Let's get out of here!'

They hopped their way out of the Sacred Glade. The air already felt fresher, though the stench of Fungellus would live long in the memory.

'. . . like rotten egg poots,' said Marvin, as they recounted the events on their way out. But they were cut short by the noise that greeted them.

They stared in amazement while chants of 'Mushrooms! Mushrooms! Mushrooms!' filled the air. Tiddlywink stepped forward to greet them.

He seemed a lot less hostile since the events at the Candyfloss Cave, though still sported the odd bit of blue floss on his outfit.

'Yes, yes, well done!' he said, turning and motioning for quiet from the crowd, who settled down in response.

'Superb work, mushrooms! No doubt you'd like to dedicate your splendid victory to your esteemed Council members, who sadly could not be with you on the front line of battle due to those hideous spores!'

He turned to face the crowd and was met with a chorus of 'BOOOO!' and 'GET OFF THE STAGE!' which was particularly memorable for the fact that there wasn't actually a stage. Even his colleagues on the council got in on the fun.

Tiddlywink went redder than strawberry laces and began to huff and splutter as Gnomedalf stepped forward.

'That's quite enough from you, Tiddlywink!' he said, and cheers rang out again. 'This victory belongs to these brave mushrooms, and Trevor's friends: Twinkle, Blossom, Herbert, and Hoofius!'

The cheers became deafening, and Trevor eagerly looked around for his pals.

'Who, sadly, could not be with us right now . . .' continued Gnomedalf. The noise quickly died down. Trevor's tiny mushroom heart went into overdrive.

'. . . as they are helping our beloved Rainbow Dragon to recover to full health!'

No sooner had he spoken, and to his surprise, the Rainbow Dragon burst out from behind the crowd, shooting through the air, spiralling and doing loop the loops as glitter fell from her wings and dusted everyone.

Trevor squinted into the distance. Doing
their best to keep up with the dragon were
the four other heroes, and Shroomsworth.

The crowd parted to let them through.

'YOU DID IT, TREVOR!' Twinkle hugged him so tight Trevor thought *his* head might pop off.

'Easy now!' said Shroomsworth. 'I haven't given him a full medical examination yet!'

But there was no stopping any of them.

Well, that seems like a nice way to wrap things up.

Pass the sick bucket.

'Great,' said Trevor, as the hugathon came to an end. 'You all slept through the one time I didn't need rescuing.'

'I feel so refreshed,' said Blossom, stretching and missing the point entirely.

'We might not be awake at all if it weren't for you and the other mushrooms,' said Hoofius. 'Denise told us all about it. I'd never have figured out how to use Fungellus's spores against him!'

'Where would we be without your big brain?' said Twinkle, rubbing Trevor's head playfully.

'Still guessing at that leprechaun riddle, most likely!' added Herbert.

Trevor grinned and felt like he knew his own strength for the first time.

'Indeed!' continued Herbert. 'I can't wait to hear all about it again over a pot of green tea . . .'

'And cake!' added Blossom. 'The one with the pink and yellow squares.' He started licking his lips at the thought.

'But first . . .' said Hoofius. 'Fungellus is gone, the Rainbow Dragon is well again, and Herbert wants to put the kettle on. I do believe we've just completed a quest . . .'

'Ahem!' Gnomedalf cleared his throat.
'Sorry to interrupt, but . . . weren't we
in the middle of something? ONE, TWO,
THREE, FOUR!'

The Happy Forest Band struck up, and the
Frolic Festival was finally back under way.

As everyone basked in the carnival atmosphere, the Rainbow Dragon fluttered in the sunset skies above, breathing new life into the tortured forest.

The remnants of Fungellus's corruption were no match for her pure rainbow breath.

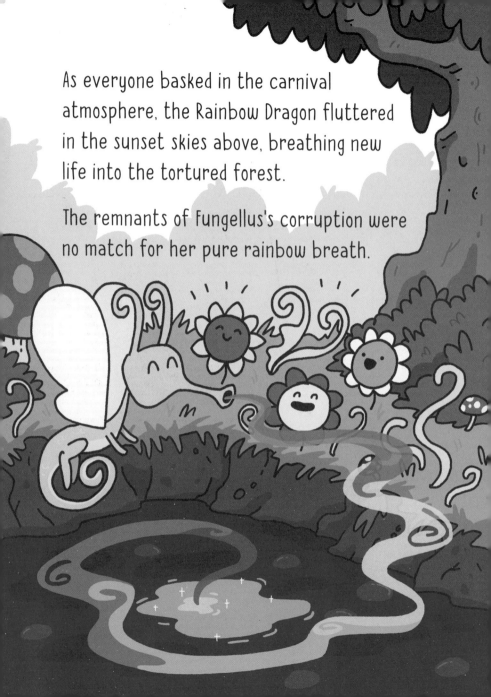

And the Mystical Crystals of Life were given new energy, to radiate through the Forest for another 100 years.

Yup. Everything seems to be in order.

With her work complete, the Rainbow Dragon returned at last to the Sacred Glade, where there was only one thing left to do . . .

177

. . . sleep.

In the weeks and months that followed, the Super Happy Magic Forest returned to more . . . everyday dramas.

Admin Bunny had endless paperwork to do.

But that's just how she liked it.

Blossom joined the Super Happy Scouts.

I will do my best!

But was kicked out for gross misconduct.

Om nom nom

Nooo! We are supposed to be selling the cookies!

Lenny thought he might be turning into a butterfly . . .

It's happening!

. . . But it was just an upset stomach.

I'll put the celebration cake away.

Dr Shroomsworth went to new lengths to secure his favourite ingredient.

Why do you keep following me?

And Tiddlywink was the lucky winner of a free spa holiday.

But it turned out to be a scam.

Gnomedalf wandered the forest, savouring life and noticing all the little things . . .

. . . like new flowers.

Beautiful!

And new flavours.

Delicious!

MATTY LONG

As a young boy Matty always thought he would grow up to be a game show host. But instead he became the next best thing: an illustrator and author! He has mostly made picture books and this is his first chapter book so he hopes you like it and want to tell everyone.

When Matty is not working, he's usually telling himself he should be working. All while playing video games.

Matty lives in Ely, Cambridgeshire, and really wants a cat.

You can find him online at www.mattylong.com